GEORGE AND MARTHA
FULL OF SURPRISES

For my nephew
Alexander Christian Schwartz

The stories in this book were originally published by
Houghton Mifflin Company in *George and Martha: One Fine Day*, 1976.

Houghton Mifflin Books for Children is an imprint of Houghton Mifflin
Harcourt Publishing Company.

www.hmhbooks.com

Library of Congress Cataloging-in-Publication Data is on file.
ISBN: 978-0-547-14421-4

Printed in Singapore

TWP 10 9 8 7 6 5 4 3 2
4500272698

GEORGE AND MARTHA
FULL OF SURPRISES

written and illustrated by
JAMES MARSHALL

HOUGHTON MIFFLIN BOOKS FOR CHILDREN
HOUGHTON MIFFLIN HARCOURT
BOSTON • NEW YORK

TWO STORIES ABOUT

TWO BEST FRIENDS

STORY NUMBER ONE

THE BIG SCARE

"Boo!" cried George.

"Have mercy!" screamed Martha.

Martha and her stamp collection went flying.

"I'm sorry," said George. "I was feeling wicked."

"Well," said Martha. "Now it's my turn."

"Go ahead," said George.

"Not right away," said Martha slyly.

Suddenly George found it very difficult to concentrate on what he was doing.

"Any minute now, Martha is going to scare the pants off me," he said to himself.

"Maybe she is hiding someplace," he said. George made sure that Martha wasn't hiding under the sink.

During the day George
got more and more nervous.
"Any minute now," he said.

But Martha was relaxing in her hammock.
"I'm sorry I forgot to scare you," said
Martha.

"That's all right," said George. "It wouldn't
have worked anyway. I'm not easily fright-
ened."

"I know," said Martha.

19

STORY NUMBER TWO

THE AMUSEMENT PARK

That evening George and Martha
went to the amusement park.
They rode the Ferris wheel.

They rode the roller coaster.

25

They rode the bump cars.

They were having a wonderful time.

But in the Tunnel of Love, Martha

sat very quiet.

It was very, very dark in there.

Suddenly Martha cried, "Boo!"

"Have mercy!" screamed George.

"I didn't forget after all," said Martha.

"So I see," said George.

JAMES MARSHALL (1942–1992) was one of the most popular and celebrated artists in the field of children's literature. Three of his books were selected as New York Times Best Illustrated Books, and he received a Caldecott Honor Award in 1989 for *Goldilocks and the Three Bears*. With more than seventy-five books to his credit, including the popular George and Martha series, Marshall has earned the admiration and love of countless readers.

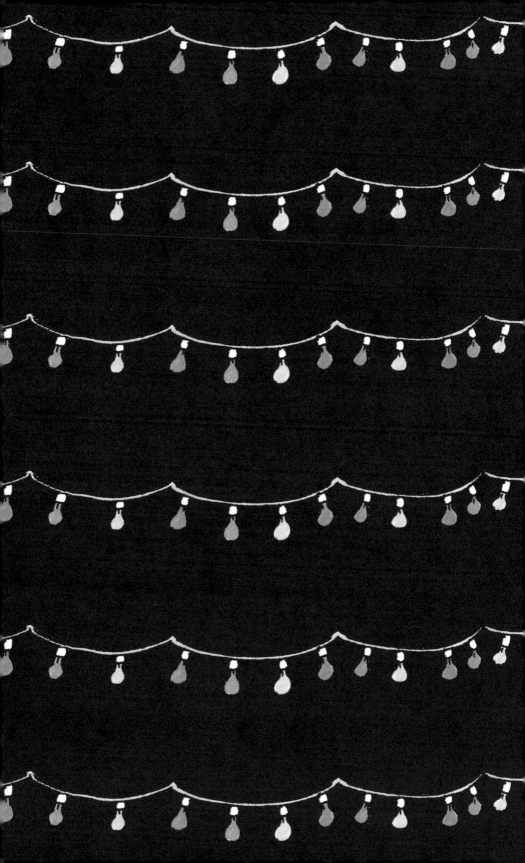